Sensati

Spring-Heeled Jack & The Disc-Men

About the author

David J H Smith was originally from Slough, Berkshire but is now living in Somerset.

He graduated from Thames Valley University with an Honours Degree in History & Geography before going on to study History at Post Graduate level at Westminster University.

David has worked in various jobs such as Immigration, Retail Manager, Facilities Officer and IT before becoming a writer and setting up 'Things From Dimension - X' which specialises in the sale of rare and collectable comic books.

Other Works:

The Titanic's Mummy

Sensational Tales

Spring-Heeled Jack & The Disc-men

By

David J H Smith

AMAZON EDITION

Paige Croft Publishing, Yeovil, Somerset

David J H Smith asserts the moral right to be identified as the author of this work

Cover Template by Jo Stroud
Cover Art 'Spring-Heeled Jack & the Disc-man' by Jo Stroud

Amazon Edition - 2020

Published by Paige Croft Publishing
Printed through Amazon

Also available on Amazon Kindle

All rights reserved. No part of this publication may be reproduced, stored in a retrieval system, or transmitted, in any form or by any means: electronic, mechanical, photocopying, recording or otherwise, without the prior permission of the publisher.

This book is sold subject to the condition that it shall not, by way of trade or otherwise, be lent, re-sold, hired out or otherwise circulated without the authors prior consent in any form or binding other than that in which it is published and without a similar condition including this condition being imposed on the subsequent purchaser

CHAPTER 1

Spring-Heeled Jack slowly started to regain his senses.

The first thing he became aware of was the pain in his head followed moments later by the fact that he was now in a sitting position, arms by his sides, tied up against a large tree. He then realised, to his relief, that he was still wearing his goggled devil mask and cowl, which covered his face- meaning his secret identity was safe; but he did note with some surprise that his shirt and jacket had been ripped open exposing his chest. His mind then registered the fact that it was still night, with the full moon high above in a cloudless sky: therefore he could not have been unconscious for very long.

Fighting the grogginess and the sudden urge to be sick, he began to try to push against his bonds, but they remained tightly in place.

"I wouldn't bother with that if I were you," said an angry female voice. "I made sure they were tied tightly so there's no getting away."

Jack looked up to see a woman walking over to him. She was of medium height and had long blonde hair and deep blue eyes. She wore a long tan dress, which was gathered in at the middle by a brown leather corset. Around her waist was a belt on which were hung a number of brown leather pouches as well as a strange looking pistol. Jack momentarily thought how strange she looked, then checked himself; after all, his clothing (which consisted of dark boots, white britches, a dark jacket with white stripes on the front with wing-like attachments underneath his arms, clawed gloves as well as his mask) could hardly be classed as normal Victorian attire.

The woman stopped a few feet away and cast her eyes over him. "So, this is the infamous 'Spring-Heeled Jack', the terror of London Town," she spat, with more than a hint of disdain in her voice. "They say you are a devil with supernatural powers, over a hundred years old, but that isn't true is it? You're just a man in a costume!"

Jack shrugged. "The papers and Penny Dreadful magazines tend to make up what they want about me. Most of it's not true."

"But the jumping part was right," continued the woman, "you must have leaped ten feet in the air. I'm presuming that there is some kind of spring type device in your boots?"

"Something like that," replied Jack evasively, "and just for the record, sometimes I can get up as high as twelve feet."

"Well, it's a shame you didn't leap that high earlier, because if so you would have missed us and we wouldn't be in the mess we are now!" She motioned over to her right. Jack turned to look at where she was indicating and saw, a short distance away, an overturned carriage on the tree lined roadside with a man next to it, wearing a makeshift splint on his leg, soothing a large black horse. The man was wearing a brown suit, high boots and around his waist was a brown belt from which hung a short sword as well as a number of leather pouches and glass vials containing different coloured liquids.

This sight made Jack recall what had happened. He had spotted the carriage moving swiftly along the road, and had decided to intercept it by jumping in front of it and then leaping out of the way at the last moment. It was something he had done so many times before with other carriages but this time something went wrong; he failed to get the height he needed, resulting in him being hit and the carriage crashing.

"I'm sorry," said Jack eventually, "I see your friend's injured."

"He's my Uncle," replied the woman. "And yes, he has a badly sprained ankle from when the trap turned over. It could have been much worse though and you have pretty much stopped our plans for tonight."

"I'm sure there will be other costume parties you can attend," noted Jack.

"Costume party?" replied the woman dangerously. "*Costume party?*"

"Er, yes," said Jack, "I presumed that by the way that you are dressed you were on the way to a party of some kind."

Anger engulfed the woman and she reached for her belt, pulling out the strange looking gun and aiming it towards Jack. She pulled the trigger and the glass tube on the top of the gun filled with light and a small blast of electricity flew from the gun's mouth and landed just above his head, scorching the bark on the tree, making him flinch. "Don't try my patience!" the woman roared.

"That's enough Sara!" called a voice, which belonged to the injured man who was now hobbling over to them.

"I wasn't going to harm him, Uncle," she

replied, as she replaced the strange looking gun to her belt. "I want to make sure he's handed over to the police alive and well."

"Actually," said the man, as he reached them and stopped, "I was thinking of an entirely different course of action." He looked down at Jack. "Greetings, my name is Samuel and this is my niece Sara."

Jack nodded.

"Alright Uncle," continued Sara, "what did you have in mind?"

"I was rather thinking he could take my place for tonight," Samuel replied casually.

"What?" cried Sara and Jack in unison.

"Yes," continued Samuel to Sara, totally ignoring Jack's horrified reaction, "there's no way I can go on this evening's excursion with my injured ankle and it's either him going in my place or we will have to call tonight off, and we might never get such a good opportunity again."

"But we can't just recruit a random person to our cause, we know nothing about him," cried Sara.

"We know he's not one of *them,*" affirmed the man, motioning down to Jack's exposed chest.

"One of who?" asked Jack.

"Look," stated Samuel, again continuing to ignore Jack, "the situation is far from ideal I grant you but his jumping and climbing ability could be useful and if the worst comes to the worst he could be used as a sacrificial lamb as it were."

Sara looked down at Jack and nodded. "Alright, there could be some benefits of using him I suppose, but can you at least let me take his mask off now? I'd like to know who exactly I'll be working with."

"No," replied Samuel gently, "we've already been over that."

"Yes, but that was *before* you decided to pair me up with him!" protested Sara.

Samuel shook his head. "Like I said, a man that protects his identity with a mask would not do so lightly so we should respect that."

Sara sighed and rolled her eyes. "Alright then," she reluctantly agreed, "have it your way."

"Good, well that's settled then," said Samuel. "Bessie," he nodded over to the horse that, on hearing her name, whinnied, "can take the both of you to the docks where you can catch up with the shipment, which in turn will lead you to Professor Kender's lair."

"What about you?" asked Sara.

"I'll make my own way home and then make arrangements for the carriage to be collected. When you've finished tonight's mission you can set our friend free and then we can work out our next move."

"Alright," said Sara, "I'm sure that …"

"Hey! Hey! You two!" cut in Jack.

"What?" asked Samuel, finally taking notice of him.

"You seem to be forgetting one minor detail!"

"Which is?"

"What happens if I don't want to be part of whatever you are planning?"

"Oh, but you do!" said Samuel knowingly.

"And what makes you say that?" asked Jack.

"Because," answered Samuel, with a smile, "a man like yourself, who dresses up in a costume and goes around at night causing mischief and stopping the occasional crime, is a man who is looking for an adventure. Well Sir, we can offer you all the adventure you could ever want!"

CHAPTER 2

In a matter of a few minutes the mysterious Samuel and Sara had completed the revised preparations that were needed for their mission. Sara now wore a small brown leather rucksack, which she had rescued from the carriage. Down one side of it hung a short whip while on the other was attached a lethal looking machete. Samuel had attended to the large black horse Bessie, double checking her over for any injuries and shortening down the long carriage reigns to make them suitable for normal riding. He then brought the beast over to the tree where Jack was tied up and Sara was now waiting. The woman took hold of the reigns, patted the horse on the side, put one foot in the stirrup and in one fluid movement mounted it.

From his belt Samuel produced the short

sword that had a chain surrounding the blade. He moved over to Jack. Pressing a button on the hilt the chain started to spin. Samuel moved the blade to the ropes which were cut instantly. Turning the chain off, he then stood back and nodded down to Jack. "Alright, get up."

Jack paused, then carefully rose to his feet and refastened his shirt and jacket, eyeing the strange looking sword. "I've never seen a blade like that before."

"I'm not surprised," replied Samuel. "It's one of a kind. Do you think you could use it?"

Jack nodded.

"Good." He moved the weapon closer to Jack so he could see it clearly. "This switch turns it on and off. I would advise you not to get your fingers in the way once it's running." He then passed the weapon to Jack who took it and tested its balance before turning it on for a few seconds.

"You'll need this as well," continued Samuel, as he took off his equipment belt and passed it to Jack. "I don't have time to go through what's in the pouches and vials. I doubt you will need them, but I'm sure you can muddle through if you do."

Jack replaced the sword into its sheath and fastened the belt around his waist as Sara manoeuvred Bessie over to him. "Climb up behind me," she ordered. He did as he was told and put his arms around Sara's waist, which was the correct way for a passenger to ride in such situations.

"Now remember," stated Samuel to Sara, "tonight is about information gathering, nothing more. Follow and observe. Do you understand? Once we know where Kender's lair is we can take things from there."

Sara nodded, and then turned back to Jack. "Hold on tight, we've got a bit of time to make up." She then flicked the reigns and tapped the flank of Bessie, who responded with a whinny and sped forward down the road.

Although Jack was used to horses, he had never ridden bareback and had certainly never been a passenger as he was now. So he found the whole experience slightly unnerving, as well as very uncomfortable. However, there were more pressing things on his mind. "Right!" he called out to Sara, "I think it's time you told me exactly what I have gotten myself into."

"I guess that only seems fair," agreed Sara, "but there is no backing out now! This is too important."

"I'm not going to back out," assured Jack, "I just want to know what I'm facing."

"Alright," she replied, slightly easing off on Bessie.

"What if I told you that a man called Professor Kender was building his own private army? And when I use the word 'building' I mean it literally. He is taking people and converting them into machines."

"I would say that the Penny Dreadful magazines are up to their old tricks again."

"Oh, I wish that were true!" replied Sara wistfully. "No, I'm afraid this is very real. The reclusive Professor has discovered a way to do it."

"But that's impossible!" cried Jack.

"I've seen the results for myself," confirmed Sara, "and they are very real. The head and hands of the subject are removed and re-attached to a specially constructed mechanical body which consists of two large metal discs from which mechanical arms and legs are attached. Of course the mechanical body is hidden under normal clothes so you have no idea that underneath is actually one of them. There are a number of these Disc-*men* in existence, including Professor Kender himself."

"Hold on, you used the term Disc-men quite deliberately," noted Jack, "are there any Disc-women?"

"From our research there doesn't seem to be," replied Sara. "He only seems to convert men. And apart from those he creates for his own private defence force, he is targeting those in positions of power; business, local government and the like. He offers them immortality in exchange for their service once the process is completed. The Professor wants to build an empire of immortal mechanical men that he will rule over."

"Has this been reported to the authorities?" asked Jack.

"We tried," answered Sara, "but it didn't go well. The story is so fantastical and I'm afraid we have a 'history'. My Uncle is an inventor and sadly, in some quarters, has a reputation for being a 'crackpot' and that, added to some of our past exploits, have gotten us into trouble in the past, so we were dismissed out of hand and they refused to take the matter any further."

"Inventor eh?" mused Jack. "Well that explains the chain-sword and your equipment."

"Yes," confirmed Sara, "he has created all manner of gadgets."

"Well it sounds to me as though you need hard evidence that these Disc-men exist," mused Jack. "What about if you were to capture one and present it to the police, then they would have no option but to take notice?"

"We did think of that," replied Sara, "but I'm afraid that each Disc-man has a self-destruct mechanism and the converts are not afraid to use it either. It seems that the Professor has some kind of hold over them and they would rather destroy themselves than be revealed. But you are right, physical evidence is the key to this, so we are trying a different approach by searching for Professor Kender's workshop where he makes these creations. We've already established it's not here in London, although where the exact location is, is proving extremely elusive."

"Which brings us up to tonight?" suggested Jack.

"Yes," agreed Sara. "The Disc-men are made out of a special kind of metal which comes from Southern Africa and we discovered a shipment is being brought into the country tonight. It's arriving at the docks at midnight."

"Ah, I see," said Jack, his mind racing ahead; "follow the shipment once it's unloaded and that will lead you directly to Kender's secret hideout."

"Exactly," replied Sara, "once we have the location we can pay it a proper visit later. The aim then is to retrieve the hard evidence as to what is going on there. We are also hoping that we can secure a list of people who have already undergone the transformation process. Although it won't be easy; the Professor knows that we are onto him and is bound to try to stop us."

Jack nodded; the overall plan was sound and could work.

"Well, now you know all about us and what we are doing, it's your turn," suggested Sara. "I don't expect you to reveal your identity but you can at least tell me why you do what you do and why in that particular costume."

But Sara's request fell on deaf ears as Jack had noticed something odd ahead of them just over to the right, by the trees that lined the road they were heading down.

CHAPTER 3

The small red rat-like body and bushy tail instantly gave itself away as a red squirrel. However, this particular squirrel seemed to be defying gravity by sitting in mid-air about seven feet off the ground eating a nut. The creature then suddenly looked up, dropped his snack, turned and disappeared into the trees.

Jack's mind leapt instantly to one conclusion.

There was a booby trap.

Someone had strung a rope out across the road which, against the darkness of night, was invisible to the eye.

Jack started to call out a warning to Sara, but it was too late.

The rope, of course, hit Sara first and she was pushed backwards into Jack as Bessie, unaware of what was happening, thundered forward leaving her two riders momentarily in the air, before gravity took over and they fell, landing heavily on the ground. Aware that whoever had laid this trap for them was likely to follow it up with an attack, Jack quickly jumped to his feet and looked around, to see three men now running towards them. Each wore dark shoes, grey trousers, a collarless shirt over which was a dark waistcoat. All were armed with what looked to be a standard police truncheon around which was wrapped copper coloured barbed wire. Jack was about to call a warning to Sara, but she had already seen the danger and, still on the ground, had reacted by drawing her gun and firing. An electronic bolt flew through the air and hit the leading thug who exploded into a blue ball of flame and disappeared, leaving nothing but a pile of ash. She tried to fire again, but the weapon had run out of charge. "Quick!" she cried to Jack as she got up, holstering the gun as she did so. "You take the one on the left, I'll take the one on the right!"

Following Sara's orders, Jack launched himself forward towards the oncoming thug, drawing the chain-sword from its sheath and turning it on; so the chain around the blade started spinning. The two men came together, with Jack swinging his chain-sword in an arc aiming to disarm his opponent, but somehow the thug managed to dodge the blow and responded by bringing down his truncheon hard onto Jack's arm.

By rights such a blow should have broken Jack's arm instantly, but the thin metal strips that had been sewn into the sleeve of the winged jacket acted like armour, protecting him. However, the force of the impact was enough to make Jack drop his chain-sword to the floor. Undeterred Jack jumped back and responded with a 'one – two' combination punch. His first target was the thug's jaw, which made the man stagger backwards. Jack then followed it up with hitting him in the stomach, but instead of making contact with soft flesh and the thug doubling over, Jack's fist smashed into something hard that responded with a metallic thud. On seeing the surprise on Jack's face the thug smiled and pulled open his shirt and waistcoat to reveal, where his chest should have been, two large round copper coloured disks, about ten inches thick, connected in the middle by a large hinged bolt. "You can punch me as hard as you like," cried the thug triumphantly, "but it won't do any good."

Jack stared at the Disc-man, his mind taking in exactly what he was seeing.

"Right!" blurted the thug, having had enough of the delay, "gawping time over – as are you!" He then started to move forward, swinging his truncheon as he went.

On seeing the attack Jack suddenly dropped to the floor kicking out in a sweeping motion as he did so, hitting the thug in the legs and causing him to fall. Quickly looking around him, Jack spotted the fallen chain-sword a short distance away and scrabbled over to it, picking up the still whirring blade. He then turned back to the Disc-man who was now in the process of getting up. Then in one movement, Jack lunged towards the man and plunged the chain-sword deep into the top disc. The blade cut through the metal and the thug slumped back to the ground. Unsure exactly how to deal with such a foe, Jack continued to ram his weapon home and the blade continued right through the Disc-man and deep into the ground, rendering him helpless. Jack switched the blade off and took a step back as he watched the thug struggle, reach for the chain-sword and try to pull it free but to no avail. Then, without warning, the Disc-man's body was engulfed from head to toe in a blue flame, which extinguished itself seconds later, leaving the chain-sword sticking up out of a pile of ash.

Recovering himself, he looked around for Sara. He saw her about twenty feet away from where he stood. She was on the floor with a thug, who he presumed too was a Disc-man, standing over her moving in for the killing blow. Jack instantly knew that there was only one course of action open to him if he was to reach her in time. He started to run forward then, utilising his special leaping ability, launched himself, sailing through the air and hitting the thug, knocking him off his feet. The two men landed with a thump a few feet away from Sara. Jack quickly sat himself up looking round to see the Disc-man lying on the ground with his head at an impossible angle but still alive, his arms and legs thrashing about as well as moaning and calling for help.

"Are you alright?" asked Sara, who had now gotten up and had gone over to Jack and helped him to his feet.

"Yes, I think so," he replied. "And you?"

Sara nodded. "Yes, thanks to you. I lost my footing and it allowed him to get the best of me," She shook her head in frustration with herself, "so embarrassing!"

"Oh, I wouldn't worry," replied Jack. "It can happen to the best of us! Besides, things worked out alright in the end." He pointed over to the Disc-man. "There you have your evidence. Come on, let's go and see what he has to say for himself." And with that he started to walk over to the fallen mechanical man.

"No! Stop!" cried Sara, as she lunged forward and grabbed Jack by the arm and dragged him back. "He won't allow himself to be taken!" Jack pulled free and was about to say something when the Disc-man, like his two companions before him, suddenly exploded into a ball of blue flame which disappeared, leaving a pile of ash on the ground.

"Well I think that makes us even," proclaimed Sara.

Jack nodded, realising that if she hadn't stopped him he would have been caught in the blast and severely injured or worse.

"Come on," continued Sara, "we need to get ourselves to the docks. If we miss that shipment there'll be no way of tracking down the Professor." She then turned, put her thumb and forefinger in her mouth and let out a long sharp whistle. A few moments later, out of the darkness, Bessie appeared trotting over to her.

While Sara attended to Bessie, Jack went back to his chain-sword and, after a few moments, managed to release it from the ground. He then moved over to the rope that was still strung out across the road to cut it down so some other traveller was not caught by it. He brought the blade down hard severing the line. Then an idea came to him and again, using the weapon, cut off a section of the fallen rope, coiled it, and attached it to his belt, before moving over to Sara who was now back on Bessie's back. As before, he climbed up behind her and they continued their journey, keeping an eye out for any further surprises that might be awaiting them.

CHAPTER 4

Jack and Sara arrived at the docks just after midnight. They stabled Bessie before continuing on foot to the berth where the steam powered cutter, which was carrying the metal for the Discmen, had docked and the contents were being transferred into a large horse-drawn waggon.

Under the cover of darkness they moved in as close as they dared, ending up about thirty feet away from the unloading, hiding behind a pile of barrels and crates which were stacked by a large recycling barge. From this vantage point they could clearly see activity by the cutter. They had arrived just in time; the men around the waggon were placing the last of the crates into it while others were preparing a large canvas sheet which would be used to cover everything over for the journey ahead.

"Right," said Jack, "that waggon is laden down pretty heavily so it's not going to be able to move very fast. It should be easy enough to follow."

"I was actually thinking of moving in closer and hitching a ride on the back," suggested Sara.

Jack shook his head. "No, that's way too risky."

Then just as Sara was about to reply, the engine of the recycling barge sprang into life as the barge's floodlights suddenly illuminated the entire area and, for the first time, Jack and Sara could see that they were in fact on a platform that was used to tip waste into the barge. Before they could react, the platform started to rise up on the left hand side and they found themselves, along with the barrels and crates, tipped over the edge of the dock into the open section of the barge, landing unceremoniously on top of a large pile of discarded metal waste about eighteen feet below. Then as they started to struggle to their feet, from the crane above them, a large heavily weighted cargo net was released, which landed spread out over the debris pile, pinning them down.

"There!" called a voice from above, "that should stop you jumping out!"

Looking up they could see a man dressed in a similar style to the thugs they had encountered earlier, smiling down at them from the dock. Sara instantly went for her belt and produced a small boomerang type weapon which she launched upwards through the netting. However, the thug easily dodged out of the way of it, partly due to her aim being hampered by her being pinned down and partly due to the wall of the barge. "Now, now!" he called down, "that wasn't very nice!"

"I'm sorry," replied Sara, "that was a bit rude of me. Let us out so we can come up and apologise to you in person."

"Not a chance," replied the thug. "Your days are numbered!" He then looked across, presumably to the bridge of the barge, and yelled, "Right-o Harold! Start her up and let's get out of here!"

"Aren't you gonna shoot'em first, Fred?" came the reply.

"Nah!" said Fred, "let the shredders do the job and let's get out of here!"

"Okay, whatever you say! You sure I can't stay and watch though?"

"Sorry, no time!" replied Fred, looking round, "shipments leaving. We gotta go. Just start her up and leave it."

"Alright!" agreed Harold disappointedly. Then seconds later, from below, there came the sound of another motor starting up, followed by a crunching sound and the pile of debris that Jack and Sara were on started moving and shifting as it was being shredded from below.

"Cheerio!" called Fred and disappeared out of sight.

Realising that they were not going to be able to move the net, both Jack and Sara reached down to their belts for edged weapons to try to cut themselves free. Jack opted for the chain-sword while Sara went for her machete. However, after a few moments, it was clear that this was no ordinary rope; woven into the hemp fibres were strands of metal.

"It's no good," cried Sara, "my machete isn't cutting through!"

"Neither is the chain-sword," confirmed Jack, as he frantically worked on part of the mesh.

"Wait a second," blurted Sara, indicating

down to Samuel's equipment belt that Jack was now wearing. "The red glass vial on your belt; it's acid, you can use it to burn your way through."

Looking down, Jack saw the small glass tube and, discarding the chain-sword, pulled the vial free from its small leather holster and carefully removed the cork stopper.

"Don't get any on yourself," warned Sara, "it will burn right through you!"

Jack nodded and carefully tipped the vial, allowing a few drops of the red liquid to drip onto the mesh. Instantly there was a fizzing sound and the rope started to dissolve. He moved to another section of the netting and then another, carefully dripping the acid onto it.

"Hurry!" pressed Sara, noting how fast the debris below them was disappearing, "we don't have much time left."

"Nearly there!" confirmed Jack, as he used the last few drops of acid before throwing the vial away. He then forced himself through the small opening he had made and, once free, stood up and launched himself into the air towards the overhanging crane, where he managed to grab onto the now empty hook. Then quickly, from his belt, he grabbed the coil of rope he had earlier taken from the booby trap across the road, and let one end drop while holding on tightly to the other.

As Jack had been doing this, Sara had been using the opportunity to abandon her rucksack and squeeze herself through the hole Jack had made in the netting. On seeing the dangling rope just above her she jumped into the air, grabbing onto it tightly, just as the recycle rollers got through the last layer of debris and started to devour the cargo net.

"You alright?" called down Jack.

"Yes," replied Sara, looking back down into the recycling barge to see the net was gone, leaving the vicious looking spinning barbs. "That was close! I had no idea recycling could be so dangerous!"

"We're not out of the woods yet," cried Jack. "I don't know how much longer I can hold on to the hook. Hold on tight! I'm going to try to throw you clear!" And with that he started to swing Sara back and forth towards the dock, with each arc getting bigger and bigger, until he was able to let go and she flew through the air, landing in a heap on its edge. Quickly she pulled herself up and turned round to look back, just in time to see Jack lose his grip and fall, disappearing from view, back into the barge's shredder. "Noooo!" she screamed, but then seconds later Jack reappeared as he used the power of his legs to leap out of the barge and landed on the dock on his side a few feet away.

Instantly, Sara scrambled over to him on all fours. "Jack! Jack! Are you alright?"

"Er, Yes, I think so!" he replied, as he sat up. "A few bashes here and there, but luckily I was able to jump clear before the shredders got me."

And with that they both slowly stood up and looked around them to realise that the dock was now totally deserted, with the Disc-men and their waggon gone and the ship that had delivered the shipment now steaming away from the docks.

"Blast it!" cried Sara in despair.

"I'm sorry," replied Jack. "On the plus side we got out alive and we live to fight another day!"

"There is a lot of 'we' going on in that sentence," observed Sara.

Jack nodded. "I prefer to see things through to the end. Besides I really don't like the idea of those mechanical men running around causing chaos and mayhem!"

"Thank you," said Sara, with a smile, "I think that we could use some help with this particular problem. Come on, I think you'd better come back to our house in London and we can work out what to do next."

CHAPTER 5

Battered, bruised, injured, but feeling very lucky to be alive, Sara and Jack returned to the stable where Bessie was waiting for them. They slowly rode back to London and arrived at Sara's town house at around seven o'clock in the morning, to find Samuel was already there waiting on the doorstep.

Once inside, Sara told Samuel about what had happened at the docks, their failure to follow the shipment and their escape from the waste disposal barge. With this done, Sara and Jack were given a chance to rest and recover from their ordeal. Jack was shown to a bedroom on the second floor where he was left in privacy to allow himself to take off his mask and costume and to clean himself up as best he could in the ensuite bathroom. Then, just as he had finished, there came a knock on the door followed by footsteps disappearing down the corridor. He slightly opened the door and peeped through the gap to investigate and found, left outside for him, a breakfast tray with bacon, eggs, toast, a pot of hot coffee, a morning paper and a hand written note inviting him to meet Sara and Samuel in the first floor study when he was ready. Gratefully he took the meal into the room where he devoured it while scanning the paper then, once finished, he put back on his costume and devil mask before heading down to the study. There he found Sara, who was now wearing a long blue dress, sitting on a small leather settee by the fire reading and Samuel working away behind a desk that was covered with papers and books.

"Good morning Jack," said Sara, as she put the book to one side and stood to greet him. "How are you feeling?"

"A little sore in places," he replied cheerfully, "how about you?"

"The same," she replied, with a smile, "but I'm more frustrated at the fact that we lost our chance to find Professor Kender than anything else."

Jack shuffled awkwardly. "Yes, I've been thinking about that. I do feel slightly responsible. If I hadn't jumped out on you in the first place you wouldn't have lost all that time in getting to the docks and things could have turned out differently."

"*Could*," emphasised Sara, "it's clear that they were expecting us from that rope across the road, and the trap of the recycling barge. The reality is that if Samuel and I had been on our own that 'different outcome' could have been both of us being killed."

"Thank you," stated Jack, "you are very gracious."

"Not at all," she replied, as she motioned him to take the empty chair opposite her.

"So," said Jack, as he sat himself down, "what's our next move? There must be some other way of getting to Kender."

"Well if there is," replied Samuel, as he limped over to the fireplace to join them, "I'm afraid that we haven't thought of it yet. The shipment was our best chance to find him and now that chance has gone."

"Perhaps there'll be another shipment at some time?" suggested Jack.

"No doubt," agreed Samuel, "but it could be months away, assuming we can even find out where and when it is. We need to find him another way, and fast."

"Does Kender have any family that he could be traced through?" asked Jack, "A wife or, failing that, a sibling or some other relation?"

"No," answered Sara, shaking her head, "the Professor doesn't have any family or friends at all; he seems to be quite alone in the world."

Jack paused and thought for a moment. "Mmm 'Professor', is that an actual title? I mean it's not a nick name or some honouree entitlement?'

"No," said Samuel, "he's a genuine Professor of engineering and science."

"Then perhaps that could be the answer," mused Jack. "Surely, as a Professor, he must be attached to an educational establishment in some form?"

Sara shook her head. "No, we've already looked into that. He was a lecturer at the Royal Polytechnic Institution, Regent Street, here in London, but resigned his position a few years ago and has no contact with them since."

"People who have reached that level in academia rarely give up all association with their area of study," pressed Jack. "Perhaps he could be found indirectly? I'm thinking of a recent paper he might have published, membership of an organisation connected to his field, even through possible monthly subscriptions of a journal or similar?"

"I'm impressed with your logic," said Samuel, with a smile, "but I am afraid that we have already thought of that and have made all the appropriate enquiries which have all come up with nothing."

"We've also tried other similar lines of enquiry but to no avail," added Sara. "The man is untraceable."

"If you can't get to Kender directly you are going to *have* to try to get to him through his creations, despite the risk of them blowing themselves up," said Jack. "His thug converts don't seem an option, but what about those who have paid to become Disc-men?"

"Well we haven't really had that many opportunities to challenge them," confessed Sara. "They, of course, don't advertise the fact they are now all but machines and these are people you cannot normally just walk up to, because of their high status positions in society."

"But what if you *could* just walk up to them?" replied Jack, an idea forming.

"I'm afraid that's just not possible," said Samuel.

"Oh, I think it could be," disagreed Jack excitedly. "There is a summer masquerade ball that is thrown at Harrington Hall, here in London, every year. In fact this years is tomorrow. The cream of society is there so it is more than possible that some of the Disc-men converts could be there as guests."

"That does sound likely," pondered Samuel.

"So, why not go to the ball itself?" suggested Jack. "Whilst there we could try to find one of the

Disc-men and, in that kind of environment with others around, they would be far less likely to try to blow themselves up; who knows we could even run into Kender himself."

Samuel shook his head. "Those types of events are invitation only, and there would be no chance of somehow sneaking in, the security would be phenomenal."

"I can get us an invitation," announced Jack confidently.

"In less than a day?" challenged Samuel.

"Just leave things with me," reassured Jack firmly. "Now, can you get the carriage up and running?"

Samuel shook his head. "No, I'll have to hire one and a horse as well to give Bessie a rest, but that won't be a problem."

"Good," said Jack, standing and moving into the room. "Then I had better take my leave. Meet me at the turnpike on the north road at nine o'clock tomorrow night, of course you will need suitable attire for a masquerade ball." That last comment was directed at Sara.

"Oh, I'm sure I can find an outfit for the occasion," she asserted.

"Good! You see, I did say there would be costume parties you could go to!" quipped Jack, referring to his comment about her costume when he had met her the night before.

"Yes, very droll," replied Sara, rolling her eyes, "and speaking of costumes, you can't leave the house and go walking around London dressed in yours. You are welcome to stay here till it gets dark, when you'll be able to sneak out unnoticed."

"I'm sorry, but there's no time," replied Jack. "I have a lot to prepare. I need to go now."

"Then we'll have to find some way to hide you." She turned to Samuel. "Do you still have that long cloak of yours?"

"Better still," said Samuel excitedly, "I believe that I have a hooded monk's robe somewhere. It would be a bit big, but could do the job."

"That would be perfect," proclaimed Sara. She turned back to Jack, but he was gone.

Looking around, to see where he was, they spotted the now the open first floor window and the billowing net curtains, indicating that their mysterious new friend had opted to take this method of exit. Moving quickly to the window they looked out to see a dark figure on the roof of the building in front of them heading away in a series of large leaps.

CHAPTER 6

Just before nine o'clock Samuel parked up a hired horse and open top carriage at the spot where Jack had instructed. Sara opened the door and stepped out into the evening air. She was wearing a bright yellow ball gown with matching yellow high-heeled shoes. Her long blonde hair had been styled into an elaborate bouffant that was adorned with jewels. Over her eyes, attached with paste, was a small Domino mask, which was also decorated with miniature gems and glitter.

She looked around for some sign of Jack, but he was nowhere to be seen.

"Do you think that he could have changed his mind?" she asked Samuel.

"More than possible," he replied glumly.

"So what do we do if he has?"

Samuel shrugged. "I guess we try to execute the plan on our own. We drive up to the house and you try to talk your way inside."

Then, without any warning, they both became aware of a figure standing next to them which seemed to appear from nowhere. The man was dressed in a jester costume consisting of an all in one baggy silk suit that was decorated in large red and yellow diamonds. On his feet were oversized curling toe slippers, while on his hands were white gloves. The man's face was covered by a grinning papier Mache mask which was set into a three pronged red and yellow jester's cowl.

"Jack, is that you?" asked Sara.

"Indeed it is!" replied Jack, as he gave a theatrical bow. "And may I say how radiant you look, even though you do resemble a giant canary."

"Yes, thank you for reminding me," she replied, annoyed. "I do have more suitable attire underneath."

"As do I," replied Jack in a more serious tone as he tugged at his costume, which hid his own 'Spring-Heeled Jack' outfit underneath. He then looked up at Samuel and nodded. "Evening! How is that ankle of yours doing?"

Samuel grunted. "It feels as though it's being stabbed with red hot needles!"

"Thank goodness for that!" replied Jack cheerily. "For a moment I thought it would still be hurting and you would hold it against me! Shall we get going?"

"I guess that will largely depend on if you have managed to get an invitation," answered Samuel.

Jack reached inside his costume and produced a small white envelope and held it up. "Here it is, all present and correct."

"Can I have a look?" asked Sara, eyeing the invitation with curiosity.

"I'd rather not," replied Jack, as he hurriedly placed it back into his costume. "Remember, time is against us. At midnight everyone is gathered into the ballroom and has to remove their masks, so we need to have our investigation completed by then."

"Alright," conceded Sara, and with that the two of them climbed into the carriage. When they were seated Samuel flicked the reigns and, with a whinny, the horse obediently moved off into a trot.

They travelled for about twenty minutes until they were forced to stop, joining a short queue of other carriages that were lined up at the large entry to Harrington Hall. At the gate each carriage was approached by a guard who checked the invitation before allowing them in.

The line slowly moved forward until it was the turn of the carriage in front of them. The guard moved towards it and spoke to the driver briefly before turning his attention to its occupant; a man dressed in a cavalier costume. As the conversation went on it was clear to Jack, Sara and Samuel that something was amiss, with both the guard and the Cavalier's voices and body language becoming more and more animated. Then, without warning, a swarm of other guards appeared and the Cavalier and his driver found themselves hauled from the carriage and taken away. Another guard took the driver's seat in the empty carriage and, with a flick of his wrists on the reigns, the vehicle sped forward through the gate and off to the side.

With the excitement over, the main guard resumed his duty and signalled to Samuel to drive forward, which he did.

"Good evening," said the guard, as the carriage stopped and drew level with him, "apologies that you had to witness that little scene a moment ago. He claimed that his invitation had been 'lost'. We have a very strict rule on gate crashers, they are not tolerated lightly!"

"So very glad to hear it!" said Jack, in a put on upper class voice, as he handed over the envelope with the invitation in it. "Have to keep the riff-raff out eh, what? I presume he'll be dealt with in a suitable manner?"

The guard opened the envelope, looked at the contents and placed both pieces of paper in a satchel which hung from his belt and nodded. "Oh, have no fear of that your Lordship. Now continue up the path to the main house please. Enjoy your evening."

"Will do indeed!" replied Jack in his false voice then Samuel, before the guard had time to change his mind or ask any questions, urged the horse onwards.

"It worked!" said Sara with relief, after they had passed through the gate. "Now, the invitation, it was a forgery wasn't it? No wait; it belonged to that poor chap in front of us didn't it? You somehow must have taken it from him earlier today? Come on you must tell us."

"No, the invitation was genuine," replied Jack and, sensing that Sara was not going to relent until she had an answer, he added. "It was actually for myself and a guest."

Sara stared at Jack in surprise and disbelief. "Hold on," she said, after the information sunk in, "he called you 'Your Lordship' that means that you …"

"I'd really rather not say any more about it if it's all the same to you," Interrupted Jack quickly. "I've always been uncomfortable with the title and don't want to give away any more information in case you guess who I am."

"Alright, whatever you say – your Lordship," replied Sara, with heavy emphasis on his title, which made Jack visibly squirm and Samuel, who was listening in on the conversation, chuckle loudly.

After a short distance Samuel pulled up in front of a stone staircase that led up to the house, where a footman suddenly appeared and opened the carriage door. Jack and Sara stepped out and were directed up the flight of stairs to the open doors of the house. As they ascended the steps Samuel was directed along the path to the coach park where he, along with all the other drivers, would spend the evening until they were required to pick up their passengers in the early hours of the morning.

At the top of the staircase Jack and Sara were greeted by staff who directed them into the main house where they found themselves in a spacious hallway. From there they were guided to the right, down a long picture gallery, before turning left into the large ballroom which was filled with people milling about in costume, both on the main floor and the two long balconies that flanked the room. At the far end of the room there was a small orchestra that was playing classical music, while waiters and waitresses were walking around with trays of canapés and champagne. On one side of the room there was a large five tier chocolate fountain. On the top of it was a large chocolate unicorn, and on the table underneath were all kinds of fruits and cakes to dip into it. While on the other side of the room were tables and chairs where some party goers had seated themselves.

"I've never actually been to a ball like this before," enthused Sara, with a hint of excitement in her voice.

"I can assure you they are overrated," replied Jack casually.

"Only if you are going to be miserable and unsociable," commented Sara with a smile and then, looking around, she suddenly started to laugh.

CHAPTER 7

"What's so funny?" enquired Jack.

"I see that there are a number of people who have been inspired by you," said Sara, noting that there were at least three people in 'Spring-Heeled Jack' style costumes ambling about.

"Pale imitations," replied Jack dismissively, clearly unimpressed.

"Oh, I don't know," mused Sara, nodding over to one of the Jacks in particular who was wearing a smart new crisp version of the devil uniform, with silver trimmings and oversized heeled boots. "He looks pretty impressive."

Jack grunted. "I'd like to see him try to climb the side of a building or take on three footpads in that dress uniform."

Sara was about to reply when a man wearing a Plague Doctor's outfit walked by them. Jack stepped forward and slapped him on the back, making him stop in surprise. "What a delight to see you here!" cried Jack in his high theatrical voice. "I thought you were still overseas. Tell me, how are things with that diamond mine of yours?"

"Er, I don't have any connections with the diamond industry," proclaimed the puzzled partygoer.

"Oh I'm sorry!" uttered Jack quickly, looking the costume up and down. "I thought it was Sir Wilbur Metcalf under there!"

"No," confirmed the man, shaking his head.

"Difficult to tell under these masks, isn't it?" said Jack.

"Yes, well that's the general idea," pointed out the man, as he nodded and walked away.

"What was that all about?" asked Sara.

"I thought he might be a Disc-man," explained Jack, "but when I slapped him on the back I didn't feel the metal disc."

"So is that your plan for this evening?" enquired Sara. "Walking up to people and assaulting them in the hope that you eventually find one of Kender's creations?"

Jack shrugged. "I'm not sure going up and asking them would work."

"Yes, well, you could be right on that," conceded Sara. "Perhaps if we split up, look around, listen into a few of the conversations; we might get a clue to who could be a Disc- man?"

"You just want to check out that chocolate fountain don't you?" replied Jack knowingly.

"I'm hungry!" she protested with a smile, "and besides, there seems to be quite a few people gathered around it."

"Well I think I'll just wander around and hope that I find out something useful as I go," stated Jack.

And with that the two of them headed off in different directions with Jack disappearing into the crowd while Sara made a beeline over to the long table where a number of ladies were chatting around the large chocolate fountain, whilst dipping food into the flowing chocolate.

At the other end of the table, Sara picked up a bowl and proceeded to fill it with some of the fruit, cakes and other goodies available. Then, looking over towards the fountain, she noticed that the large decorative chocolate unicorn on the top had moved slightly and was very likely to fall. Before she could say or do anything one of the costumed ladies suddenly stepped back and banged hard into the table making it jolt; which was enough to dislodge the chocolate sculpture. As the unicorn tumbled downwards towards the table it hit the flowing chocolate sending streams out over the women around it, making them scream. Sara quickly put down her bowl and went over to help. However, as she reached them, her high heeled shoes landed on a patch of spilt chocolate on the floor which caused her to slip sideways and she landed heavily face down on top of all the dipping foods. As she lay sprawled out on the table, out of the corner of her eye, she became aware of the chocolate fountain itself swaying, no doubt unbalanced by her impacting the table.

Then the machine started to fall …

Meanwhile, Jack had ended up in the small group of men dressed up in elaborate Judge Costumes who were discussing a contentious matter of the day.

"He is a genius, a national hero," said the first Judge. "I feel his adventures should officially be recorded into one commemorative chronical and sold in every book shop and on every newsstand. My publishing firm would happily do it!"

"I might have known," said the second. "Any profit to be had and you'll be there! No, hang him!

Hang him high! Hang him long! He's a menace to society, not some hero."

"Catch the blighter and stick him in jail and forget about him," protested the third.

"Too harsh!" insisted the fourth. "Admit him to Bedlam. Any man who dresses up as some sort of devil-bat and parades around at night the way he does must have an unbalanced mind. He needs urgent, caring, compassionate, medical help; electro-shock treatment, freezing cold baths, long periods of isolation and of course enforced fasting."

"I'd throw in a swift beating or two as well!" put in the second Judge. "It's the only way to deal with the young pup!"

"I hear that he's actually helped a few members of the public," put in Jack finally, after hearing enough. "Only last week he stopped a vicious mugging and what about the report that he saved that girl who fell into the Thames?"

"I bet the scoundrel took her money afterwards!" said the third Judge.

"I'm sure he didn't!" cried the first Judge, who

had originally rooted for Spring-Heeled Jack. "You are just making that up. You are being way too harsh on this man, whoever he is."

"Agreed," said Jack quickly. "For every one negative story about him there are two positive ones as well as another three absurd ones."

"And who precisely asked you for your opinion?" asked the fourth Judge, looking Jack up and down. "This is a private meeting for gentlemen! Be off with you, you clown!"

"I'm not a clown, I'm a Jester," replied Jack and, before he could stop himself, he added. "I think the only clown here is your good self, and as such you could at least have the courtesy to be funny!"

"What! How dare you!" said the Judge, turning towards him. "I have a good mind to take my glove off and slap you around the face and you know what that means."

"You want to duel with me?" spluttered Jack, trying not to laugh. "Alright, you may have the sword and pistol while I will take a rolled up wet newspaper. I guarantee you'll be wiping newsprint off your face for a week!"

A look of sheer anger crossed the man's face and he was about to remove his glove when a female voice interrupted the proceedings.

"There you are!"

The Judge stopped and Jack turned to see Sara standing next to him, her yellow dress and hair covered in chocolate and bits of cake and other confectionery.

"What happened to you?" blurted Jack, looking her up and down trying not to laugh.

Sara paused. "The short answer is - it was a unicorn."

"Um, but, what?" Stammered Jack, confused.

"Never mind," she said, as she grabbed him by the arm and pulled him away from the slightly bemused group of Judges, only stopping when they were a safe distance away. "What on earth are you doing?" she scolded him. "Are you trying to start a fight and get yourself taken off by the police?"

"Trust me," replied Jack, "people don't get arrested at these kinds of dos. Besides, you should have heard the things they were saying about me, well not me personally, Spring-Heeled Jack."

Sara rolled her eyes. "I wouldn't have thought you would be the type to be thin skinned. More importantly were any of them Disc-men?"

"I'm afraid I couldn't tell you for sure," replied Jack sadly. "How about you, did you have any leads before your unicorn intervened?"

"No. I guess we'll have to split up and try again," confessed Sara, "perhaps if we focus on the waiting staff? They could give us a lead, especially if we pass them some money."

"Actually I don't think that will be necessary," replied Jack, as something on the first floor balcony had grabbed his attention. "Take a look at that," he said, motioning upwards.

CHAPTER 8

Sara did as she was asked. Upon looking up she saw a man dressed as a highwayman, who was leaning on the side of an empty bath chair, talking to another man who was dressed up as a Bishop.

"I recognised that bath chair," continued Jack. "It belongs to Robert Basset, son of Lord Basset."

"You know them?" asked Sara.

"Know of them, would be more accurate," replied Jack. "But what I do know is that Robert was involved in an accident when he was a boy; he fell from a tree. The result was total paralysis from the waist down, and yet there he is standing up."

"Being turned into a Disc-man would certainly allow him to walk again," said Sara, as she watched the Bishop leave and Robert return to the chair.

"I think I read something in the society pages of the Times about Robert having some long term experimental treatment," continued Jack.

"Well that's one way of describing the conversion process, I suppose," replied Sara, with a smile. "I guess that's their cover story for him suddenly being able to walk again."

"Yes I think you're right," agreed Jack. "Come on, let's go up and have a chat."

"What if he tries to blow himself up?" asked Sara.

"Oh, don't worry about that," replied Jack, "he wouldn't dare!"

And so with that Jack and Sara moved across the ballroom and up the staircase to the first floor and then over to Robert who, on seeing them approach, started to pull himself upwards from his bath chair.

"Oh don't get up on our account!" insisted Jack. "After all, we don't want to overuse those new mechanical legs of yours, do we?"

"What?" gasped Robert in surprise, as he let himself back down again. "I have no idea what you are talking about!"

"Oh I think you do," ventured Jack, as he quickly moved behind the chair, grabbing the handles that stuck out of the back, and started to turn it round. "Come on, I think we should go for a little ride and then a chat."

"No stop, you can't do this, I'll .."

"Self-destruct? You do and I guarantee everyone will know about your Father's secret offshore accounts," proclaimed Jack, glancing over to Sara who nodded approvingly.

"But, but, wait!" protested Robert. "You can't do this!"

But it was too late and Jack propelled the bath chair along the balcony, with Sara in tow. Turning left down a corridor they were confronted with a number of doors, which were each tried in turn. They were all locked, except for the last one which opened to reveal a music room, identifiable by the fact there was a piano, a harpsichord and two single-action harps.

Jack pushed Robert inside and into the middle of the room and Sara followed closing the door behind her. Then grabbing a nearby chair, wedged it under the door handle ensuring they would not be disturbed. With no-one else around there was no need to continue the pretence, so Robert stood up abandoning his bath chair.

"A remarkable recovery," commented Jack.

"Yes, well, I did have some help," admitted Robert. "But it seems that you know that already."

Jack moved over to Robert and reached out his hand, placing it firmly on his chest feeling that it was metal rather than flesh.

"I could open my costume if it helps," offered Robert obligingly.

"No, that won't be necessary," replied Jack, removing his hand and standing back. "I already know what a Disc-man looks like."

"It's not the most pleasing aesthetic is it?" reflected Robert. "It's pretty crude if you ask me, but it does the job. There are plans to create an outer layer of skin to cover the discs themselves, but that is some way off yet, but I'm sure that Professor Kender will manage to do it."

"We're hoping to stop him so it doesn't get that far," ventured Sara.

"You won't be able to," said Robert, with a smile. "I won't let you." Then, without warning, he turned and grabbed his bath chair and swung it round hurling it in the direction of Jack and Sara. He then ran to the door that led to the terrace, opened it and stepped outside, then jumped over the balcony rail disappearing from view. Jack and Sara, dodging round the bath chair, quickly followed. Arriving out on the balcony they looked over the edge and could see the figure of Robert, who had landed safely some twenty feet below. He was now running across the lawn away from the house.

"Time to change!" said Jack, as he removed his jester hat and mask throwing them aside to reveal his normal 'Spring-heeled Jack' mask and cowl. He ripped open the jester costume and cast it to one side to expose his familiar striped jacket and white britches. Finally he kicked off his curled slippers that covered his leather boots.

He then jumped onto the stone balustrade. "Come on," he called to Sara, "I can get us down safely using my wings as a parachute! But you'll have to change first!"

However, Sara had other ideas.

She too jumped quickly onto the balustrade then stepped off it. As she dropped, her large dress inflated and slowed her descent. She landed safely on the patio below where she climbed out of her oversized ball gown to reveal leather boots, brown trousers, complete with a thick leather pouched belt, and a brown leather corset over her cream shirt. She then tore off her mask and let her blonde hair down, shaking it loose.

While Sara was in the process of changing, Jack leapt from the balcony. He threw his arms out as he did so, allowing the loose material underneath to catch the wind creating a wing-like effect, which slowed his descent. He landed on the patio next to her. The two of them set off across the grounds as fast as they could after Robert, rapidly closing the gap between them. Then somewhere to the left there came the sound of a gun being fired and the crackle of an electrical beam. Jack was hit first, his whole body tensed up which caused him to fall to the floor. Before Sara could react, there was another whooshing sound and she too was hit by an electrical beam and felled. Both tried to move, but their limbs would not respond, and they remained helpless on the grass.

From out of the darkness appeared two huge men, both carrying large static rifles. Jack and Sara recognised the first instantly as Fred, the thug from the recycling barge. "Well, well, well!" he said, "look what we have ourselves here Harold."

"I said back on the barge you should have shot them!" replied Harold. "Still, never mind!"

Jack tried to speak, but found he couldn't.

"Oh, I wouldn't bother if I were you," stated Fred. "That blast will keep you still for a good while."

Then Robert appeared, realising that his pursuers had been neutralised. "Thank you, thank you," he gasped to Fred and Harold. "They jumped me! They seemed to know all about my conversion. I ended up jumping out of a first floor window to escape! I knew the Professor was here and was at the Summerhouse so that's where I was making for. I thought if I could lead them to him, I'd find help."

"You did the right thing," confirmed Fred reassuringly.

"Yeah," agreed Harold, "you can leave things with us now. We'll take things from here. You get back to the party and enjoy yourself."

Robert nodded and, with a final look down at Jack and Sara, quickly headed back towards the house while Fred and Harold moved in and disarmed Jack and Sara. Then the two thugs picked up their prisoners, slinging them over their shoulders, and started the short walk across the grounds to the edge of the lake where the Summerhouse was located.

CHAPTER 9

It did not take long for Fred and Harold to arrive at the glass Summerhouse. They opened the door, stepped inside, and dropped Jack and Sara unceremoniously to the floor. With the effects of the electrical blast slowly wearing off they managed to sit themselves up and look around to see that there was some kind of meeting taking place.

The man in charge of the proceedings, Professor Kender, was dressed up as the Devil. Only this costume was much more elaborate and sophisticated than Jack's; with a long black silk cloak which partially covered his red three piece velvet suit and black leather shoes. Instead of a mask his face had been teinted red with make-up, which made his actual black goatee beard and eyebrows stand out all the more. His dark black hair was slicked back and on the top of his head, attached by a band, were two large red horns. Directly in front of the Devil was a man dressed head to toe in bandages, clearly masquerading as an Egyptian Mummy. Between them was an elderly Disc-man, with his clothes on the floor in front of him. Over to the side was a small table on which there seemed to be a number of legal documents and official looking stamps.

The Devil glanced over to Jack and Sara and smiled. "If you will bear with me for a moment," he said, in a polite deep voice. "We are just going over some last minute details of our latest recruit. We have just completed some improvements to the design that our friend here could benefit from, should he so wish." He then returned his attention to the Mummy. "Well? What do you think? Do you like this upgraded version of our design?"

The Mummy surveyed the Disc-man in front of him before nodding. "And you say that with this body, swimming will be easier?"

Kender nodded. "Yes, much. The arms and legs are now hollow allowing twenty five percent more buoyancy. Of course, you will still have to wear a 'cover all' bathing suit if you decide to go out on a public beach, but a small sacrifice."

"That would be good," noted the Mummy thoughtfully. "I do like a good trip to the beach."

"And of course being generally lighter it will make riding easier and more comfortable for you and, of course, your horse."

The Mummy nodded, his body language indicated that he was interested.

"Improvements have also been made to the joints giving even more durability, as well as to the 'stomach' area which means that any food and drink you consume will just dissolve into nothing and you would not have to manually empty the cavity on a regular basis."

"And you personally have this body?" asked the Mummy.

"Indeed," replied the Devil, tapping his chest which made a dull metallic sound. "Once it was perfected I of course had one made for myself, partly to test the product, and I can assure you it is well worth it! You are the first paying client to be offered this new 'Mark II' and all the benefits that come with it."

"I'm presuming that there will be an extra cost?" asked the Mummy warily.

"A small one, yes," said the Devil, with a sly smile, "I understand that you have a small retreat in Devon?"

"My cottage?" gasped the Mummy in surprise. "You want my cottage as well as the agreed fee of half my fortune to become a Disc-man?"

The Devil nodded. "There is a lot of extra work involved in making this particular version and the metal is especially expensive to find and import. Of course, if you don't want to that's up to you."

"Could I think about it and then upgrade later as you did?" asked the Mummy.

"Of course," said the Devil. "The only issue is that there is a limited amount of the new material available to me at the present time. If you decided to pass on this offer, others will snap up this opportunity and I'm not sure when I could offer it to you again."

The Mummy paused and then nodded. "Alright!" he enthused, not wanting to miss out, "I'll do it. I'll go for the upgrade."

"Excellent!" cried the Devil, as he clapped his hands together. "You have made the right decision! Now if you could accompany my man Dennis here, he will complete the final paperwork and we shall be on our way! Everything is prepared and waiting for you. By this time tomorrow the conversion will have taken place and the next phase of your life will begin!"

The Mummy stood aside and the Disc-man, Dennis, quickly retrieved his clothes from the floor and started putting them back on as the two of them headed across to the table, while the Devil moved across the Summerhouse to stand over the captured Jack and Sara. "So, what do we have ourselves here?" he asked, regarding the pair. "I would hazard a guess the infamous Spring-heeled Jack himself and the constant thorn in my side of

Miss Sara Latimer. I presume that means your uncle is nearby."

"What do you think?" she replied sarcastically.

"Good," said the Devil, with an evil smile. "Harold, Fred!"

"Yes, Professor," replied the thugs together as they stood up straight to attention.

"Go and find our old friend Samuel, and make sure he never bothers us again."

"No!" protested Sara.

"Once he's dead, take his body and bury it deep in the wood. Make sure the grave is deep and unmarked."

"No! No!" cried Sara.

"Oh, and feel free to rifle through his pockets and keep whatever you find for yourselves. Think of it as a bonus!" added the Devil casually.

"Yes, Professor, thank you Professor," replied the duo in unison, and with that the two Disc-men left the Summerhouse to carry out their murderous task.

"You evil heartless monster," vented Sara. "If I wasn't tied up …"

"You would try and attack me and you would find yourself stunned again. Now," he said, moving forward, "I am curious. Let us see who the infamous Spring-heeled Jack really is." He reached out to the struggling Jack and took hold of his Devil mask and in one movement pulled it off to reveal a dark haired man in his early thirties, clean shaven, with brown eyes.

The Devil stared down at Jack.

Unable to hide her curiosity Sara also found herself drawn to look at the mysterious man who had become her companion.

The Mummy and Dennis, with the legal papers now signed, moved over to the small group and too stared at the unmasked man before them.

Jack looked around and smiled as he saw the quizzical faces looking at him.

"Well!" cried the Devil, "who are you? What is your name?"

Jack smiled; it seems that the fact that he had kept a low profile in his real life, keeping himself out of the society pages and the like had paid off, as no one seemed to know who he was. Realising, with relief, his identity was still safe he smiled and said, "I'm nobody. Let's just leave it at that."

Angered, the Devil lunged forward and punched down, landing a blow on Jack's cheek. "I said who are you?"

Jack recovered himself, looked up and smiled, remaining silent.

"Alright then," said the Devil, realising that he was not going to get his answer. "If that's the way you want to play it, so be it." He then turned to Dennis. "Right, go get the carriage, I think that it's time we were on our way."

"Very good Sir," he replied, "what about these two?" He nodded towards Jack and Sara.

The Devil smiled. "Oh they will be coming with us!"

CHAPTER 10

As instructed Dennis fetched the carriage. Jack and Sara, with the effects of the electrical blast now completely worn off, were loaded into the back where the Professor and the Mummy also took their seats. After leaving Harrington Hall, via a back entrance, they travelled west for the rest of the night; first along the main roads, and then turning off onto a series of tracks which led into the countryside. They stopped once in the middle of the night to allow the horses to rest for a short time and allow everyone to stretch their legs.

As daylight broke, the carriage veered right onto a hidden track where it continued for another mile along what looked like an abandoned road until it came to a covered wooden bridge that spanned a dry river bed. The bridge was guarded by two Disc-men who were manning a giant static gun placed on a small platform.

"Welcome to the lost village of Henwick," announced Kender, as they crossed the bridge and moved past the guards, turning right down a small track. "It was abandoned about eighty years ago. It seems the draw of an expanding London and the opportunities it offered were just too much for the residents to resist. They left in dribs and drabs until there was no one left and the place became forgotten; you won't even find it on any modern maps. It is the perfect location for me to live in peace and carry out my work."

Jack and Sara exchanged a quick glance. The

remoteness of the location explained why the Professor could not be found, but more importantly they realised that here would be the place to retrieve the evidence they needed regarding the existence of the Disc-men and Kender's activities, assuming of course they could then escape with this information and make it back to the outside world afterwards.

The carriage continued onwards heading directly into the village centre which surrounded a well maintained green. In the middle was a large pond where several ducks were swimming. Around the village green was an array of grey stone thatched buildings. To the north was a road lined with cottages that led up to a large church, which had a strange metal structure on its tower.

The carriage circled the common and stopped outside what appeared to be the tavern, where upon they were greeted by an elderly Disc-man with a long white beard. "Good morning, Professor!"

"Good morning Morris!" replied Kender. "Has everything been prepared?"

"Indeed it has Sir," replied Morris, looking directly at the Egyptian Mummy. "We're all ready and waiting."

"Good, good," said Kender, with a smile, "our new recruit here has decided to opt for our newer body version, but Dennis will give you all the details."

In response, Dennis jumped down from the driver's seat and opened the carriage door, indicating to the Mummy to get out, which he did before slamming it shut again.

"Now," said Kender, as he climbed into the driver's seat and picked up the horses reigns. "We shall come back to check on the progress in a few hours. I would like you to make sure that *everything* is ready and prepared for our return. Do you understand? *Everything.*"

Morris gave a sly smile and nodded, glancing momentarily at Sara.

"Good," said Kender, with a smile, "in the meantime, I could do with some breakfast and there are a few things I would like to chat about." Jack and Sara exchanged a worried glance and the Mummy was ushered towards the Tavern by the two Disc-men. Kender flicked the reigns and urged the horse onwards continuing past the green and up a small road towards the church. At the church they took a right and continued onwards until eventually they arrived at a large three storey

Manor House. He stopped the carriage outside the main door, jumped down and motioned to Jack and Sara to follow, which they did. The Professor then went to the door which, as he reached it, was opened by a bald headed Disc-man. "Good morning sir, I trust you had a good evening?"

"Yes indeed Jenkins, very good indeed," replied Kender, as he crossed the threshold of the door with Jack and Sara following.

Jenkins eyed Jack and Sara suspiciously.

"If you could, please show our guests to the dining room," instructed Kender. "I will quickly change out of my costume and join you all in a moment."

"Indeed, Sir," replied Jenkins.

"Good!" said the Professor. He then headed towards the staircase in the middle of the hall while Jenkins motioned to Jack and Sara to follow him. The three moved over to the dining room, where Jenkins opened the door and ushered them inside.

The room itself was oak panelled and dominated by a long wooden table that had three places set for breakfast, indicating that Kender already had guests; one at the head of the table, presumably for the Professor, and another either side of him. Over to the left was a large sideboard on which there were a number of silver covered trays from which hot food would be served.

"If you could both sit on the right hand side of the table," instructed Jenkins. "I will lay new places. I'm sure the Professor and the others will be here shortly."

"Others?" asked Sara.

"Yes," replied Jenkins, with a sly smile, "*others.*" He then motioned for them to sit down, which they did, and then the Disc-man butler moved to a sideboard and proceeded to take out plates and cutlery to lay the extra places required. Just as he had finished, the door to the Dining room opened and in walked Professor Kender, now changed out of his devil costume and theatrical make-up and instead wearing a countryside tweed suit and boots. He paused, and then stood to one side to reveal the two 'others' that would be having breakfast with them.

The creatures stood around five feet tall and were covered from their bald pointed heads to their webbed fingers and toes in dark green scales.

They had small button noses and their eyes were oval in shape and were a deep amber colour.

"What on earth!" gasped Jack in surprise, as he looked at the strange creatures in front of him.

"Ah, but that's just it!" replied Kender, relishing the look of surprise on their faces, "my friends here are not from earth. They are aliens from a crystalline asteroid hidden in our solar system."

The two aliens smiled.

"I am Valtor," said the first.

"And I am Vantel," said the second.

"They can speak our language!" exclaimed Sara in surprise.

"Oh yes, indeed," replied Kender. "They are very quick learners. They and their companions learnt the basics of our tongue in a matter of weeks. In fact they have almost worked their way through my extensive library, and are even getting to grips with other languages, such as Latin."

"Companions?" queried Jack. "There are more of them?"

"Yes, there are six of us in total," answered Valtor in a soft voice.

"There should be eight of us," said Vantel sadly, "but two of our number did not survive."

"What do you mean?" enquired Jack.

"I will explain everything," said Kender, "but please, let us sit and begin to eat. I am famished."

Jack and Sara nodded and the Professor and the two aliens moved to the table, Kender taking the head seat while the aliens took the two other vacant seats. At once Jenkins appeared and in front of the creatures placed a plate of a green mush, which the Professor explained to be consisted of crushed vegetables; which was the only food from earth their bodies could process. Jenkins then proceeded to serve normal food for everyone else; toast, eggs, bacon, sausages and potatoes, which he dished out in large portions before placing coffee and tea on the table. When he had finally finished, he moved to the side and stood to attention, waiting for any further instructions or to serve up more food or drink if required.

"Please dig in," asserted the Professor, motioning to the plates in front of them. "Now, I am sure you have a number of questions. Many of them can be answered with the tale I am about to tell you."

CHAPTER 11

"It all started," said the Professor, "about two and a half years ago. Firstly, you must realise that although my background is in Science and Engineering I have an abiding interest in the natural world and I am a keen Lepidopterist, a collector of butterflies and moths. Now, it just so happened that there was a report that a rare luminescent moth had been seen somewhere in this local area. Eager to add it to my collection I ventured out late one night to try to find it. I spent hours scouring the countryside for it but with no success and so, defeated, I started my long journey home. As I was travelling back I heard, in the sky above me, a strange roaring noise. I looked up and in the darkness could just make out a strange cigar shaped sky ship heading directly downwards towards me. The ship crashed into the ground. There was an explosion, and I can remember being hit by something, and then nothing. I awoke much later here in Henwick, in the abandoned tavern, flat out on a table surrounded by my new friends here."

He pointed to the aliens who smiled back and nodded. "Of course, the surprise of seeing these creatures were nothing compared to when I realised that my body was gone, replaced by two large discs and mechanical limbs. It transpired that I had been injured terribly by debris from their crashed vessel. The creatures brought me here and, seeing the extent of my wounds, fashioned me this new strange body which they attached to my head in order for me to survive, and so the concept of 'Disc-men' was born!"

"A concept which you seem to have continued," accused Sara. "How many more of you are there?"

"In total, including my small 'workforce' and myself, eighty four, eighty five if you are going to include our friend the Mummy, who is currently being created," replied Kender. "But this is set to increase. There are a number of people in the process of raising the required funds I charge for the conversion."

"Immortality to those who can afford it," intoned Sara pointedly.

"More of a means to an end," replied Kender, with a smile. "There is a certain expense involved, but the profits generated are diverted to a much more important purpose."

"Which is?" asked Jack, his interest tweaked.

"To fund the rebuilding of the creatures space craft," replied Kender.

"We want to go home," Valtor said simply.

Jack and Sara looked to the strange creatures, both suddenly feeling certain sadness for them, realising they, and their companions, were stranded here on earth far from their home.

"We were only here on an exploratory mission," explained Vantel. "We need to return to our world."

"But won't your kind try to find you when they realise you are missing?" asked Sara.

Valtor shook his head. "It may be many decades before they realise we are lost."

"So why not just try to send a message back and have them send a rescue party?" asked Jack. "Surely that would be easier than trying to rebuild the ship itself?"

"We have tried," said Kender. "As you may have noticed there is a large antenna on the village church tower, but our efforts were in vain, so them travelling back is the only option."

"Alright," said Jack, his opinion now shifting towards Kender now he was aware of the man's motives, "but why try to do this all yourself and in secret? We have been visited by creatures from another world! This is momentous, the authorities need to be informed and what's more, with them on side, they will make available all resources required to get them back home."

"Your innocence and naivety are misplaced," said Kender, with a smile.

"Is that an insult or a compliment?" asked Jack.

"Whatever you want it to be!" replied Kender. "I have done everything I can to keep my alien friends here a secret and with good reason. If they are discovered by the wider world, they will not be helped to return home. Their craft will be taken and studied and the technology used for goodness knows what, and as for the creatures themselves," he looked across to Vantel and Valtor, "they will be taken away and studied, doomed to spend the rest of their lives in laboratories; however long that is. I'm sure that the powers that be would be more than interested in dissecting them to see what their internal structure is like."

"No, I'm sure that wouldn't happen," said Sara. "The creatures would be helped. I agree that we would want to find out more about them and any technology they have, but it would be done through friendship and understanding."

"No it would not," insisted Kender.

"You cannot say that with certainly," argued Jack.

"I can," disagreed Kender sadly. "You see, it has happened before, and I have seen it first-hand!"

"What?" cried Jack and Sara together in astonishment.

"I said it has happened before, with our Martian neighbours," repeated Kender. "They landed here in England about twenty years ago as I understand it. The creatures made contact with those in power and well, let's just say the human race did not cover itself in glory. As I have already described, their technology was captured and studied and the Martians ended up dying. Their bodies were dissected and then their remains placed in glass jars."

"How do you know all this?" asked Jack.

"Because I was called upon by the government, due to my special skill set and experience, to examine some of the technology," replied Kender.

"No, this is impossible," protested Sara, trying to take in what they had been told. "If something like that happened we would know about it, it couldn't be kept hidden."

"But it has been," insisted Kender. "Oh, there have been rumours and stories about nothing that is provable. The only substantial indication is the leap forward in technology we have seen over the past few years."

"You mean what is being dubbed 'The Industrial Revolution'?" asked Sara.

Kender nodded.

"But if that technology has helped advance mankind," reasoned Jack, "isn't that even more reason to work *with* these aliens? There has to be a way to protect them and develop anything they have to offer. Think how they could transform the world!"

Kender laughed out loud, and both Valtor and Vantel made strange noises that were similar to chuckling.

"What's so funny?" asked Jack.

"You are!" replied Kender. "That is exactly what is happening and what we are working towards here in Henwick."

"I'm not sure I totally understand you," said Sara.

"Our original mission was to secretly visit earth and to report back to our superiors," explained Vantel.

"And even though our visit has not gone as planned," elaborated Valtor, "that report has been finished and we can conclude that Earth, and those on it, are indeed more than suitable."

"Suitable for what?" asked Sara warily.

"Suitable to be taken over and ruled under our laws," replied Valtor.

"You want to invade Earth?" cried Jack in disbelief.

"Indeed," confirmed Vantel excitedly. "It will be easy enough, especially now that the groundwork is in place."

"Yes," continued Valtor, "thanks to the guidance of the Professor here, a number of Discmen have been created and are in key positions of power in your society. They will be more than sympathetic to our cause."

"You've sold out your country and your planet to these creatures?" cried Sara angrily to Kender.

The Professor nodded. "Yes, and it was not as difficult as you think, especially with the rewards I have been offered for my help and advice, but enough of this talk," replied Kender, noting that the aliens and Jack and Sara had finished their breakfast. "I think it is time that I gave you a full tour of Henwick and show you all that goes on here."

CHAPTER 12

Professor Kender led Jack, Sara and the two aliens out of the Manor house and, opting to walk rather than take a carriage, headed down a small track that stopped outside the grounds of the church.

They entered through the arched Lych-gate and headed across the small graveyard to the building itself where, from inside, they could hear movement and a flurry of activity.

"I think we might be a bit early for the morning service," noted Sara.

"On no," replied Kender, as he reached the large wooden door, "no services take place here; they haven't for a long time. When the village was abandoned, the church deconsecrated it; this is no longer holy ground." He then pushed the door open and the small group headed inside.

Looking around, Jack and Sara could see that the nave of the church had been cleared of all the pews and in their place a large workshop had been established. There seemed to be a flurry of activity with Disc-men working at various benches. To their right, it could be seen that the church tower had been opened up and standing upright in that space was the large cigar shaped space ship and just in front of this, off to the side, were two large wooden vats.

"Oh my goodness!" cried Jack, as he took in the sight of the craft. Sara's reaction was similar, staring at it in wonderment.

"Yes, it's a thing of beauty isn't it?" replied Kender proudly. "As you can imagine, the project of re-building the alien craft has been a herculean effort. We are literally trying to build this alien technology from scratch, with no plans or schematics. If that is not hard enough things are made all the more difficult by the fact that the ship's engineer, who understood the mechanics of the craft, was one of those who perished in the crash."

"If that's the case," asked Sara, "how do you know it will fly and will actually work?"

"We have run a number of small scale tests and have even fired up the engines," replied Kender. "It will work. In fact it is believed that with some additions, that we have made using earth technology, it will be better than the original!"

"So what's in those vats?" asked Jack, as he pointed to the two giant wooden casks by the spacecraft.

"That is the ship's fuel," replied Kender. "We have made our own version using combustible oil, derived from vegetables and corn. It took a year to recreate and perfect. The batch you see before you is in the final stages of the natural fermentation process."

"So that must mean that you are nearly ready to launch?" reasoned Jack.

"I would say within two to three weeks," agreed Kender confidently. "Once the fuel is ready, all that remains is to remove the communications antenna at the top of the church tower and then it is a matter of waiting for the right weather conditions. Vantel and Valtor will undertake the journey which should take just over three months, but they should be in communication with their home-world after two. By the time they arrive home, arrangements for the clandestine take-over of earth will be well under way!"

Jack and Sara glanced at each other worriedly.

"Oh come, don't be like that!" said Kender, with a smile. "The coming of the aliens heralds the coming of a new dawn for mankind."

"Whether mankind wants it or not?" asked Sara.

Kender smiled, choosing to ignore her comment. "Now, I think we have spent more than enough time here. I want to show you our main laboratory where my Disc-men are created."

With the two aliens opting to stay behind to help with some technical difficulty that had recently presented itself with their ship, Kender, Jack and Sara left the church and headed down the road towards the village green. Circumnavigating it, they arrived at the tavern where, led by Kender, they entered.

Inside, Jack and Sara could see that, like the church, the normal interior of the building had been stripped and in its place a cross between an operating theatre and a tool maker's workshop had been created. Along two of the walls ran a large workbench, above which was a range of tools and off to one side there was a small forge and an over-sized anvil, where a Goliath of a Disc-man, well over six feet tall, was working away on a piece of metal.

In the middle of the room was a large wooden operating table around which were two more of the aliens and a number of Disc-men, who were busily working away on something.

"How is our Egyptian friend doing?" asked Kender.

"Very well," replied one of the aliens, moving to one side to reveal that, laid out on the table, was a Disc-man with a shiny new body and bandages wrapped around the neck and wrists where the living flesh had been attached to the metal body, "the conversion went smoothly."

"Good, Good," said Kender, turning to Jack and Sara. "He must be about the only person in history to have less bandages after the operation than he did before! He should wake up in an hour. He will spend the next week with us recovering and getting used to his new body before returning home. Of course he will need to return to us here from time to time for routine maintenance and checks, but all machines need checking on a regular basis don't they?"

As he was speaking there was a sudden flurry of activity around the operating table. The newly created Disc-man was transferred onto a nearby trolley which was taken out of the room via two double doors, while another Disc-man appeared with cleaning equipment and proceeded to wipe down and sterilise the operating table. Moments later the doors opened again and another Disc-man appeared pushing a large wheeled frame that was covered by a sheet, which was carefully moved into position behind the operating table.

"Now," said Kender excitedly, "it is time to show you a project that I have been working on for a long time, and one that I can now at last carry out." He turned to the Disc-man by the frame and nodded. In response he took hold of the sheet and pulled it away to reveal a new mechanical body, but one with two additions to the top disc that clearly marked out the figure as a female.

"As you may have already realised," Kender started to explain, "only Disc-*men* have ever been created. However, that is to change. I desire a partner; someone who I can spend eternity with." He then turned and looked straight at Sara. "I have decided that you shall have that privilege! A woman of your calibre and spirit will make a perfect companion!"

A look of sheer horror filled Sara's eyes. "No, never, I would never …." Then, before she could finish, four Disc-men swooped in, two grabbing Sara while the other two grabbed and restrained Jack before he could do anything to help her.

"Prepare her for the conversion process!" cried Kender gleefully.

The Disc-men responded instantly by hauling Sara towards the large operating table where, still struggling, she was lifted up and then slammed down upon it. As this was happening Kender looked over towards the Goliath, who had now abandoned his work. "You, get those ropes and that half size anvil." He then turned back to the Disc-men holding Jack. "Take our friend here outside, tie him up tightly and throw him into the village pond. I want him drowned!"

CHAPTER 13

The two Disc-men holding the struggling Jack, followed by the Goliath, burst through the tavern door and out onto the village green, where they marched directly over to the large duck pond. Once there, Jack was thrown to the ground and pinned down while the Goliath, having dropped the mini anvil, moved in with the length of rope to tie him up. However, Jack was not going to let himself be such an easy victim so, as the giant Disc-man got closer, he managed to lever himself up and kick out with his legs. Jack hit the Goliath in the chest with both feet using all the power he would normally use for his mighty leaps and the Disc-man was launched backwards twelve feet into the air before crashing down to the ground, landing in a heap. This attack caught both of the other Disc-men off guard and allowed Jack to launch another onslaught, first punching one in the face, bloodying his nose, and elbowing the other. Then, using the opportunity his attack created, he scrambled to his feet and started to sprint away. But his bolt for freedom was short lived as he suddenly felt something extremely heavy hitting him in the back and he was brought down hard to the floor. Slightly stunned he looked around to see the mini anvil by his side. He realised that the Goliath, using his mighty strength, must have thrown it at him and then, before he could react, the giant Disc-man himself was upon him, hitting him hard in the jaw and yelling obscenities. Then the two other Disc-men appeared and joined in the battle. Jack found himself totally overwhelmed.

"You can fight us as hard as you like!" called the Disc- man with the bloody nose, as he was struggling with Jack's left leg. "It won't do you any good! You are going for a sleep with the fishes whether you like it or not! Hey, what the? This doesn't feel right." The Disc-man then pulled hard on Jack's foot. His boot, along with the limb above the knee, came free and right out of Jack's trouser leg, which made everyone stop.

"You went and yanked his leg off!" cried the Goliath in surprise.

"Yeah I did, didn't I?" said the Disc-man, looking at the artificial limb he now held. However, it was clear that this particular limb was no ordinary false replacement that an amputee would have; the lower leg itself seemed to be one large piston which was attached to a mechanical knee joint.

The other Disc-man, still holding Jack, reached down and grabbed at the other leg. "Hey, this one's false too!" He then pulled at the limb and in a few seconds that one was also removed from Jack's trousers. This leg was shorter with no knee joint but, like the first, consisted of a large piston.

"Well that explains how he can jump so high," said the Goliath.

"Yes it does, doesn't it?" said the first Disc-man, quickly wiping the trailing blood from his nose. "Well it looks as though you have been in the wars haven't you?"

"More than you'll ever realise," replied Jack, his mind instantly flashing back to the battlefield and the cannon blast that ended his military career and altered his life forever.

"Pretty good workmanship," continued the Disc-man with the bloody nose, looking closely at the leg he was holding. "Who made it?"

"A friend," replied Jack evasively.

"Good to have friends isn't it?" replied the Disc-man with a smirk. "A good one of mine died recently. You stuck a fancy mechanical sword in him." He then punched Jack hard on the jaw as revenge. "And this one's for my nose." He punched Jack again, but this time in the stomach.

"So what do we do with him now?" asked the Goliath. "Shall we tell the Professor?"

"What for?" said the Disc-man. "The decision's been made. He's got to die. He doesn't get a free pass just because he's had a tough time and half of him is missing. It just makes our job a lot easier. C'mon, bind him up!"

Jack tried to struggle again, but with his legs gone it was no good and within a few minutes he found himself bound with his arms against his sides. Then another rope was tied around him and the other end was attached to the mini anvil. The Goliath and the two Disc-men, one of whom had decided to take Jack's limbs with them, moved to the edge of the pond. Then Jack found himself airborne before the weight of the anvil pulled him down into the water and, just as he disappeared under the surface, he managed to take in a huge gulp of air.

"Don't forget your legs!" cried the Disc-man with a laugh, as he threw Jack's false limbs after him.

The anvil landed upright at the bottom of the pond, some fifteen feet below. Jack found himself floating above it, tethered by the rope. He then became aware of his false legs slowly drifting and landing on the pond bed a few feet away from him. Aware that he had a limited amount of time before he would black out through lack of oxygen, he started to struggle against the ropes. When he was being bound he had managed to expand his chest and push his arms out slightly to the side meaning he had not been tied up as tightly as he could have been; this had created some slack for himself, but not much.

Frantically Jack shifted his body from side to side, his strategy was to try to manoeuvre the ropes over his head, but although they did move it was not by much. Then, looking down, his eyes landed on the anvil and the horn at the end that metal workers used to fashion curves and bends in metal, and an idea came to him. Carefully he lent forwards and, flicking his body and the stumps of his legs, managed to turn over completely before propelling himself downwards. He caught the ropes on the anvil's horn and he proceeded to use it as a lever to get a portion of the ropes upwards and over his shoulder. Then, with this section of his restraint gone, Jack instantly found it much easier to move and within seconds he had freed himself totally from the ropes and the anvil.

With his lungs bursting for air he started to swim upwards but, fully aware that the Goliath and Disc-men were most likely waiting for him just in case he somehow managed to escape, he stopped himself just under the pond's surface. Then tipping his head back he very carefully pushed his mouth upwards through the water so he would not be seen and quickly took in a few gulps of air. Once his lungs were full, using his arms, he propelled himself downward and then swam back to the bottom of the pond to where his mechanical legs were waiting for him. Picking up the slightly shorter limb, Jack proceeded to fix it back onto his right leg, and moving down again he grabbed the other leg and reattached that to the stump on his left leg. After checking that the limbs were firmly in place, he tested each piston in turn, and found to his relief that both were undamaged and were still working. With this done he swam back over to the anvil where he positioned himself so he was standing on top of it. Now with a firm base below him he readied himself, and propelled himself upwards. A few moments later he exploded out of the water.

CHAPTER 14

"And here he is!" cried the Goliath. "I thought you might be tricky enough to escape! Well get yourself a load of this!" The giant Disc-man then produced a large static gun which he started to aim at Jack who, in response, was about to dive back under the water, when both men got distracted by a loud crackling sound overhead. Looking up they could see that, from somewhere behind the village, a solid beam of purple electricity was being shot into the air, which seemed to be focused in the sky above them. Around the village green doors immediately started to open and the residents of Henwick started to appear to investigate the strange phenomenon, including from the tavern where Professor Kender himself emerged. He gazed up at the beam of light, before quickly making his way over to the Goliath, to try and find out what was going on.

Seeing his chance Jack quickly swam to the side of the pond and hauled himself out of the water then, in a wide circle, started to make for the still open tavern door.

"Quick! Get him!" came the sudden cry from Kender, as he spotted Jack out of the corner of his eye.

The Goliath, his static gun still drawn, started to shoot. Jack somehow managed to evade the electrical beams and made it to the tavern, entering and quickly slamming the door shut behind him. Looking down he saw the key to the door was still in the lock so he turned it, locking himself inside before looking around to assess the situation.

Sara was now strapped to the wooden table and over her mouth was a mask that was attached to a large cylinder filled with anaesthesia, which was being monitored by one of the aliens. Standing over her, holding a large scalpel, was the Disc-man surgeon, with two other Disc-men assistants in attendance. They had all stopped what they were doing, distracted by Jack's dramatic entrance.

"You leave her alone!" cried Jack, as he took a step forward.

"I don't think so!" cried the surgeon defiantly. "Stay where you are or the girl gets it!"

Jack instantly stopped and, before he could say or do anything more, from behind him was the rattle of the door handle as someone tried to open it, but of course it remained shut. There was a pause and then there were three thumps as static beams smashed into the door's lock, no doubt fired by the Goliath.

"Give it up!" cried the surgeon. "You can't possibly get out of this alive!"

"Not a chance!" cried Jack, as he readied himself, realising the only option open to him was to use the power of his piston loaded legs to catapult himself forward before the surgeon made his move on Sara. He was about to carry out this plan when there was a splintering sound from behind. Turning he could now see the door had been kicked open and there, with a look of anger spread across his face, was the Goliath who again raised his gun. Jack reacted instantly by turning round, launching himself forward and grabbing the Goliath's arm pushing it to one side and slamming it into the door frame, causing an electrical blast to be discharged upwards into the ceiling. The giant Disc-man swore and then jabbed his other fist forward, hitting Jack in the face and causing him to stagger back, but somehow he still managed to keep his grip on the Goliath, pulling him into the building.

The two men now grappled and fought, moving around the entrance of the room in some kind of strange dance, the giant Disc-man trying to aim the static gun at Jack's head while he in turn tried to push it away, doing his best to kick out at the Goliath's legs to trip him up, but to no avail.

Then the gun went off again; the static bolt flying across the room. This sent the two Disc-men assistants into a panic and they both abandoned their posts, disappearing through the internal double doors at the back of the building to safety.

"Stop! Stop this at once!" cried the Surgeon desperately.

Jack and the Goliath ignored him and the two stumbled towards the operating table. Then another bolt from the gun went off, this one flying over the table narrowly missing the alien operating the anaesthesia equipment who only escaped by throwing himself to the floor, knocking the cylinder over as he did so. This in turn caused the face mask to be ripped off of Sara, stopping the slow supply of gas being fed to her. The surgeon, on seeing Sara was no longer attached to the cylinder, tried to stop the fight from getting any closer to him and his equipment by grabbing the side of the operating table and pushing it hard across the floor. The table smashed into Jack and the Goliath taking them by surprise and knocking them off balance, resulting in another electrical charge being released from the gun. The stray shot streaked directly across the room and hit the waiting Disc-woman's body, which exploded in a large blue flash. The Surgeon, who was standing nearby, was caught in the blast setting off his internal self-destruct mechanism, also reducing him into a pile of ash.

This commotion allowed Jack to break free and to land a devastating right hook on the chin of the Goliath, who then crumpled to the floor unconscious. Satisfied the giant was no longer a threat, Jack turned his attention to Sara, noticing as he did so that the alien who was operating the anaesthetic equipment was now scurrying away on all fours across the room to safety. Quickly he moved to the table and gently started to shake her by the shoulders. "Sara, Sara, c'mon, wake up, we've got to get out of here!"

Sara groaned and her eyes flickered open. "Jack? Is that you?"

"Yes, it's me," he replied with relief, on hearing her voice.

"What happened? What's going on?" she asked wearily, her mind still foggy. Then a look of horror crossed her face as she remembered her situation. "My body!"

"Don't worry, you are alright," assured Jack as he started to untie the leather straps that held her down. "I managed to get to you before they did anything. The drugs they gave you will wear off in a few moments and you'll be fine."

"Oh, you're all wet," she said, slightly confused as she noticed Jack's dripping clothes. "Hold on, weren't you being drowned?"

"I'm afraid I had other ideas," he replied. "I managed to escape, helped by the distraction of the electrical beam being fired into the sky."

"What electrical beam?" she replied "Where did it come from?"

"I've no idea," said Jack with a shrug, as he finished untying the last strap. "All I know is we need to concentrate on getting out of here and fast. Are you alright?"

"I think so," replied Sara, as she sat up. "What a mess," she added, as she noticed the devastation around her.

"A stray shot hit the Disc-woman's body," explained Jack. "I presume it set off the self-destruct mechanism."

"What!" cried Sara angrily, instantly realising the implications. "He put one of those things in that body? That means he could have gotten rid of me at any time he wanted!"

"Um, well I guess his idea of 'partner he could spend eternity with' had its limitations," replied Jack with a shrug. "C'mon, let's get out of here." And with that Sara got off the table and she and Jack stepped over the unconscious body of the Goliath and made their way through the open doorway stepping back into the village, stopping mid-way across the green to take in the sight above them.

CHAPTER 15

Although the strange electrical beam was now no longer being fired into the sky, its effects were clear to see. A large mass of purple tinged clouds had formed over the village and the surrounding area and, within the cloudbank, small electrical charges could be seen going off at various points, followed by low rumbles. The whole atmosphere in the village had also changed; the air seemed heavy and muggy and it was noticeable that there was no sight or sound of any birdlife around.

The Disc-men who had gathered on the green were talking and looking concerned about the strange phenomenon around them. Professor Kender, who had now noticed Jack and Sara's presence, marched over to them pointing his finger accusingly. "This is all down to you, isn't it?"

"This has nothing to do with us," replied Jack, holding his hands up. "If you remember, I was in the pond and Sara was about to be turned into one of your mechanical freaks."

"No!" cried Kender, shaking his head. "I don't believe you! This is somehow your doing! Now tell me what you did and how to stop it!"

Then, before either Jack or Sara could reply, there came the sound of a horse and, turning round, they could see a carriage being driven at speed onto the green, which pulled up sharply allowing the driver to jump down.

"You!" cried Kender angrily, seeing the identity of the driver. "You! Yooou! Yooooou!"

"That's right," cried Samuel, as he moved over to them. He smiled over to Sara and nodded to the unmasked Jack. If he was aware of who Jack was he gave no indication that he did.

"How did you escape my Disc-men?" asked Kender.

"They were no match for me I'm afraid," replied Samuel, with a wide grin, "but they were very helpful. They were so sure of themselves they wanted to tell me all about Henwick, your alien friends and your plans to take over the world by stealth, before they killed me. Of course it didn't end up going their way so after I dealt with them I grabbed my carriage and here I am!"

"And this?" said Kender, pointing to the sky.

"A minor skirmish with the guards outside the village," explained Samuel dismissively. "The mounted static gun ended up getting locked firing upwards. It's nothing to worry about."

However, as Samuel finished speaking, there was a large flash of light which momentarily illuminated a large section of the clouds, followed by a loud crack of thunder. Then another section of cloud lit up and there was a pause, and a few seconds later more thunder.

"Wow!" said Jack, in awe and amazement, "I've never seen a storm like this before."

"I'm not surprised," replied Kender. "The gun that caused it was part of the armaments on the alien spaceship. There's no telling what effects there will be!" He then looked over to the Tavern, as something caught his eye. Emerging from the door was the Goliath, still slightly dazed. "Here! Over here!" cried Kender and pointed to Jack and the others. "Get them! Finish them off!"

The Goliath gathered himself, nodded and started to make his way forward, but suddenly stopped dead, a look of horror and confusion spreading across his face. He fell to his knees and then he exploded in a blue flash and was gone, leaving a small mound of ash behind. Then there was another blue flash from the other side of the pond as another Disc-man spontaneously exploded, followed by another and another.

"What's happening?" cried Sara.

"The atmosphere the storm is causing is interfering with the internal self-destruct mechanism!" cried Kender in alarm. "My Disc-men! My beautiful Disc-men!"

Now, all around the green there was panic and the Disc- men started to run in all directions, some of them exploding as they went. High above, the sky was filled with lightning and, as the accompanying roar of thunder was unleashed, another bolt was released, but instead of staying in the sky it hurtled downwards, hitting the failed communications antenna on the top of the church tower.

The lightning instantly set the metal structure ablaze then, following the lightning rod that was designed to protect the building from just such a strike, flames travelled down the side of the tower to the ground setting the side of the building on fire. After a few seconds there was a creak and the antenna, weakened by the intense heat, toppled sideways, smashing down onto the church roof which then also was set ablaze.

Through the chaos one of the aliens appeared. He pointed to the church in alarm. "Look! Look what's happening!"

"I know!" cried Kender. "I'm not blind you know, I can see it!"

"Well do something!" said the alien.

"Like what?" asked Kender angrily. "In case you hadn't noticed our workforce is exploding around us as we speak!"

"I don't know," replied the alien, "but if something's not done fast, that fire will reach the fuel vats and that will mean the end of us all!"

A look of horror crossed Kender's face, followed by a look of hatred and contempt towards Jack, Sara and Samuel. "Come on!" cried Kender to the alien. "There might still be time to vent off the fuel into the brook that runs behind the church, it will carry it clean away." He, along with the alien, set off towards the church, dodging the still exploding Disc-men as they went.

The entire sky lit up and another bolt of lightning was released downwards, but this one landed on the roof of one of the houses near the church, which instantly burst into flames. There was a pause and then another house, just outside the green, exploded as that too was hit.

"We need to get out of here," cried Samuel.

"And fast!" said Sara

"Agreed!" added Jack.

The three of them made for the carriage where Jack and Sara jumped in the back. Samuel retook his place in the driver's seat and urged the horse onward, turning the vehicle around and heading away from the village.

With the storm still raging behind them they hurtled down the track and, after what seemed like an age, they arrived at the edge of Henwick. They sped past the now destroyed electrical cannon, which had presumably exploded due to intense overheating, and across the covered bridge where, safely on the other side, Samuel brought the vehicle to a halt.

Moments later a large lightning bolt hit the bridge and the entire structure collapsed in flames cutting the village off from the outside world forever.

There was a mighty explosion which shook the ground and in the distance, in the direction of the village, a massive fireball erupted into the air, and then disappeared as a large mushroom cloud took its place.

"That must have been the fuel vats in the church exploding," observed Sara.

"Taking the entire village with it," added Jack.

"Looks like the threat of Kender and his alien friends is over then," said Samuel, with more than a hint of relief in his voice. "There's no way anything could have survived that."

"But what about the Disc-men he already created?" asked Jack. "They can't just be left running around loose."

"I can't see them being able to do much harm without Kender and the aliens to lead them," replied Samuel, with a shrug. "We might as well just leave them be, unless of course they decide to cause any trouble." He then looked Jack up and down. "You know it wouldn't take much for me to make a few additions to that costume of yours; a utility belt, blasters on the arms, as well as making those wings under your arms bullet proof. I could even add night-vision to your goggles on the mask, if you like."

"A parting gift for my help with stopping Kender and his Disc-men?" asked Jack.

"I'm thinking as more of an investment for Sara and myself," replied Samuel. "You do seem to have proven you are more than capable and I do have a number of, shall we say, 'side projects' where you would be most useful - assuming of course you are interested."

Jack smiled and nodded. "Oh, I'm interested alright. After all, you did promise me all the adventure I could ever want and I have a feeling you can more than keep up your end of the bargain!"

Historical Notes

Spring-Heeled Jack actually existed. During the 1800's there were various sightings across England and even Scotland, of a person / persons dressed up in the devil costume causing chaos and other mischief.

Professor Kender and his Disc Men, however, are a work of fiction. They first appeared in Planet Comics #28 which was published in January 1944 and have been adapted for this story.

Spring-Heeled Jack, Professor Kender and his Disc-men are Public Domain characters.

Printed in Poland
by Amazon Fulfillment
Poland Sp. z o.o., Wrocław